UNCLE LEO'S ADVENTURES at the West Pole

Yannets Levi has written books and for television. Born in Israel to a family of storytellers, he remembers being surrounded by stories ever since he was a kid, told by his parents, uncles and aunts.

His Uncle Leo's Adventures series is one of Israel's most popular children's book series and has sold more than 450,000 copies in Israel alone. The series has also been published in the Czech Republic, South Korea and Japan. He has also written another children's book, *Mrs Rosebud is No Monster*, and two books for adults.

Yaniv Shimony is a graduate of the Bezalel Academy of Art and Design in Jerusalem, considered the top art school in Israel. After completing his studies, he worked as Art Director in some of Israel's largest advertising agencies. Currently, his work focuses on illustrating children's books. In 2008, Shimony won an award for Children's Book Illustration from the Israel Museum for his work in *Uncle Leo's Adventures in the Romanian Steppes*.

Other Books in the Series:

Uncle Leo's Adventures in the Romanian Steppes
Uncle Leo's Adventures in the Siberian Jungle
Uncle Leo's Adventures in the Swiss Desert
Uncle Leo's Adventures in the Sahara Forests

UNCLE LEO'S ADVENTURES
at the West Pole

Yannets Levi

Illustrated by Yaniv Shimony
Translated by Margo Eyon

RED TURTLE
RUPA

Published in Red Turtle by
Rupa Publications India Pvt. Ltd 2014
7/16, Ansari Road, Daryaganj
New Delhi 110002

Sales centres:
Allahabad Bengaluru Chennai
Hyderabad Jaipur Kathmandu
Kolkata Mumbai

First published in Hebrew in 2011
This edition copyright © Yannets Levi 2014
Illustration copyright © Yaniv Shimony 2011
Translated by Margo Eyon

This edition published by arrangement with Asia Publishers Int.,
Israel (asia01@netvision.net.il) through Writer's Side, India

This is a work of fiction. Names, characters, places and incidents are either the product of the author's imagination or are used fictitiously, and any resemblance to any actual persons, living or dead, events or locales is entirely coincidental.

All rights reserved.
No part of this publication may be reproduced, transmitted, or stored in a retrieval system, in any form or by any means, electronic, mechanical, photocopying, recording or otherwise, without the prior permission of the publisher.

ISBN: 978-81-291-3482-0

First impression 2015

10 9 8 7 6 5 4 3 2 1

The moral right of the author has been asserted.

This edition is for sale in the Indian subcontinent only.

Printed at Parksons Graphics Pvt. Ltd., Mumbai

This book is sold subject to the condition that it shall not, by way of trade or otherwise, be lent, resold, hired out, or otherwise circulated, without the publisher's prior consent, in any form of binding or cover other than that in which it is published.

For Michal, the One and Only
—Yannets and Yaniv

Contents

Introduction	ix
Uncle Leo Forgets Everything	1
Uncle Leo, Half-Man-Half-Woman	20
Uncle Leo in Professor Scientifani's Lab	40
Uncle Leo Dreams On and On and On	62

Introduction

Sometimes I think I'm no good at anything. Okay, maybe I'm not bad at *every*thing, but I'm not good at lots of stuff. If you ask me, my little sister has the most fun. She's still a baby. No one tells her when she does things wrong. And even when she's completely wrong, people only get excited about her.

But every time *I* don't manage to do something, my big brother laughs at me. Every time I fail at something, he says I have a tiny brain. That really upsets me. Mom says I'm talented, and that I need to believe in myself and not listen to my brother. Dad tells me that I'm a great kid. But of course they're my parents, so they try to encourage me.

When I told Uncle Leo that I'm not good at a lot of

things, he said, 'You have to know how to fail.'

'What do you mean?' I asked.

'Not everyone has the talent to fail!' he said, and Uncle Leo probably knows what he's talking about, because he has had adventures all over the world and knows lots of stuff.

Uncle Leo comes to visit us every Wednesday. Uncle Leo isn't any ordinary uncle. My mother once said, 'Uncle Leo isn't the kind of uncle you find every day. He's the finest vintage!' On Wednesdays, when Uncle Leo comes over, he tells me all about his adventures at the West Pole. And now I'm going to tell you these stories. I swear that everything I tell you is true. I didn't make any of it up. I heard it all with my very own ears, straight from Uncle Leo.

And by the way, if you don't know—my name is Andy, my big brother's is Graham, and my little sister's is Phoebe. My father's name is Eliot, my mother's is Daphne and my Uncle Leo's—as you might have guessed—is Uncle Leo.

Uncle Leo Forgets Everything

On Wednesday, my class put on a show about road safety in front of the whole school. I was supposed to get up on stage at the end of the show and say, 'Let's follow the safety rules together!' My part wasn't very big, but the teacher said it was really important because it actually summed up the entire show. All week long, I sat with Mom and memorized the words that I was supposed to say. I also repeated my line over and over at the rehearsals.

But on Wednesday, during the show, I didn't notice when it was my turn to get on stage. Everyone was waiting. My teacher quickly came over to me and whispered, 'Andy, you have to go up there.'

I got on stage, stood in front of the whole school, opened my mouth and…I couldn't remember what I was supposed to say. At first I remembered 'safety,' but the longer I stood there, the less I remembered—until eventually I couldn't remember anything at all! I just stared at the audience. Everybody was waiting for me to say something. A few kids laughed. My brother Graham was one of them.

My teacher leaned over, got close to the stage and whispered to me, 'Let's follow…', but I was so nervous I couldn't hear what she said. Finally, she took the microphone and said the line instead of me. Everyone in the audience laughed and I ran away. I ran and ran and ran, but in the end I reached the school fence, and there was nowhere else for me to run. So I went back to the classroom. I was so ashamed! I just wanted to disappear. Everyone in my class was mad at me for forgetting my part and ruining the show. And it didn't help that my teacher tried to calm them down, and calm me down too.

On the way home, Graham said, 'What happened to you? You learned that line all week long—and in the end you couldn't remember it?'

'I forgot it.'

'How could you forget? Even I remember it.'

'I remember it too, now!' I said. 'But I forgot when I was on stage.'

'You made such a fool of yourself,' said Graham. I had nothing to say.

Uncle Leo came over to our house that afternoon. Graham was at soccer practice and Uncle Leo and I sat on the balcony.

'Andy,' said Uncle Leo, 'is everything all right?'

'Actually, no,' I said.

Uncle Leo said nothing, but I could tell by his eyes that he wanted to know what was wrong.

'We put on a show at school today. I had one line to say, but when I got on stage I forgot everything.'

'You forgot everything?' said Uncle Leo. 'Completely everything?'

'Everything. I couldn't remember anything.'

'That happened once to me too,' said Uncle Leo.

'When you were in a show?' I asked.

'No,' said Uncle Leo. 'It happened when I was visiting Hole Mountain at the West Pole.'

'Hole Mountain? What happened to you on Hole

Mountain?' I asked.

'I forgot everything. I'll tell you about it,' said Uncle Leo and began. 'Once, when I was visiting the West Pole, people told me about Hole Mountain. They said that this mountain had an endless number of holes and pits, and that if you searched inside them, you could find many treasures. Immediately, I decided to set out for the mountain. I took supplies with me for the way: a map, walking shoes, a canteen of water, a hat, and sour pickles in case I got hungry. I really wanted to find some treasure. But when I reached Hole Mountain, I found that there were quite a lot of holes and pits in it, and I didn't know which hole or pit I should search in.

'I decided to try my luck. I looked in one pit and was happy to find a gold coin inside. *If there's a gold coin in the first pit, there must be many more treasures in Hole Mountain,* I thought to myself. I put the coin in my pocket and went on searching. I went from hole to pit and from pit to hole, but I didn't find anything else. Both the pits and holes were dark and empty. But when I peered into the eleventh pit, I saw something—a giant chest. I went down into the pit until I reached the chest. I opened it and discovered that it was full of big, shiny

gold bricks. I danced for joy on the spot! I had found a tremendous treasure! The chest held so much gold that it would make several people enormously rich. But that was actually the problem,' said Uncle Leo.

'What problem?' I asked. 'It sounds amazing to me! So much gold!'

'Too much gold! The treasure was too big. I tried lifting the chest, but it didn't budge. I tried pushing, shoving, dragging, pulling. No matter how hard I tried, I couldn't move the chest of gold even an inch. The pit was deep and steep, and the chest was heavy.

'I thought, *If I can't take the whole chest with me, at least I'll take one gold brick.*

'I tried to pick up one of the bricks.

Although the brick was small compared to the whole chest, I couldn't lift or move it, either. It was so heavy. I didn't know what to do. What's the point of finding treasure if you can't take it with you?

'I thought and thought until I came up with an idea. *I'll return to the city and come back with a tractor or wagon and ropes,* I thought. *Then I'll be able to pull the chest out of the pit!*

'I climbed out of the pit and stopped suddenly. I realized that this wasn't going to be easy,' said Uncle Leo, raising his eyebrows.

'Why not?' I asked.

'I looked around and saw an endless number of holes and pits. Each one of them was different from the others, but they also looked quite alike. If I went to the city and came back, I wouldn't know which pit had the treasure in it. The pit with the treasure looked very similar to all the other pits. *I must mark the pit with the treasure so I'll be able to recognize it when I get back,* I thought. I looked around and saw a large blue rock at my feet. *Great! Here's the solution! I'll put this blue rock at the* entrance to the pit. *When I return, I'll know that the treasure is in the pit next to the blue rock.* And that's what I did. I laid the rock at the entrance of the pit and started walking back to the city.

'I was afraid I would forget the mark I had left, so I kept repeating to myself, "The pit with the blue rock. The pit with the blue rock. The pit with the blue rock." I was so immersed in my chanting that I didn't notice a little pit right in my path. I stepped into it, and fell to the ground. I hit my head and passed out!' said Uncle Leo, holding his head, as if the bump he had got on Hole Mountain still hurt.

'Uncle Leo,' I said worriedly, 'what happened to you after that? How long did you stay there for?'

'I don't know how long I lay there. I was unconscious, after all. I only know that a girl found me—a little girl named Puja. She was wearing a tattered dress, dirty and full of holes. She wasn't expecting to see anyone sprawled like that in the middle of the path. She understood that something bad had happened to me. She came up to me and shook me a little until I opened my eyes.

"'Excuse me,' Puja said. "Do you need help?"

'I answered her with a yell—"Bah!"

"'Did you hit your head?" asked Puja.

"'Bah!" I answered.

"'What's your name?" asked Puja.

"'Bah!" I shouted in response.

"'Where do you live?" asked Puja.

"'Bah!" I cried.

'No matter what the little girl asked or said, I answered "Bah!"'

'But Uncle Leo,' I said, 'why didn't you answer everything the little girl asked you?'

'Because I had lost my memory when I hit my head. I forgot everything. I forgot my name, where I came from, and where I was going. I forgot how to talk. I forgot how to walk and how to eat. I forgot what people are and what animals are. I forgot that I was Uncle Leo. I forgot all my adventures. And, of course, I totally forgot about the blue rock and the treasure. The only thing I could do was lie there and yell "Bah!"

'Fortunately, Puja realized that I needed help. Even though she was small, she gathered her strength, sat me

up, and dragged me all the way to her parents' house. But actually, Andy,' said Uncle Leo, crinkling his eyes, 'I'm not so sure I would call their house a "house".'

'Why not?' I asked. 'What was special about their house?'

'The mother, father and daughter lived inside a cardboard box on the side of the road. They were very poor. They were paupers. They had almost nothing. They didn't have a television or an oven or a telephone. They had no tables or chairs or couches or rugs. They didn't even have any pictures. They just had one cardboard box that they lived in. Each one of them had only one thing to wear. Puja's torn dress was her only set of clothing, and

that's why it was so tattered and stained. The dress was full of holes, but Puja didn't have a needle and thread. So she patched up the holes with pieces of chewing gum she found on the street. Of course, she didn't have the money to buy chewing gum!

'When Puja got home, she said to her parents, "Mama, Papa, this man needs help." She meant me.

'"Help? Why should we help him?" asked the mother. "Last month, you brought home a cat without a tail, and it ran away because we didn't have any scraps to give it. Last week, you brought home a stray dog, and it left because we didn't have any food to give it. And now you're bringing home a whole person?"

"'A whole person,' said the father angrily, 'and a pretty fat one at that!'"

"'We don't have anything to eat!' said the mother. 'How are we supposed to help him?'"

"'Don't worry,' Puja told her parents. 'I'll share my food with him. I'll take care of him.'"

"'Get him out of here!' said the mother."

"'Wait a minute,' said the father. 'I see that he has sour pickles. Maybe he'll let us eat some of them?'"

'The father came up to me and asked, "Are you willing to let us eat some of your pickles?"'

"'Bah!' I said."

"'I'm sure he means to say yes,' said the father."

"'And we'll give him some of our food, right?' asked Puja."

"'No way!' cried the father."

'Fortunately for me, Puja didn't listen to her parents. Every day, she gave me half of what she ate. Every day, Puja and her parents ate one potato. They would cook it over an open fire, split it into three equal portions, and eat it with a sour pickle. Every day, Puja would give me half of her portion of the potato and half of her piece of pickle. But she didn't just give me food. She also reminded

me,' said Uncle Leo.

'What do you mean, "reminded you"?' I asked.

'She reminded me about everything I had forgotten. Every day she taught me things I had forgotten.

'First, I couldn't remember how to eat. I tried putting the food into my ear instead of my mouth. Puja fed me, and slowly I remembered how to eat.

'Then I couldn't remember how to walk. I just crawled on my back. Puja pulled me to my feet and taught me how to walk all over again—step by step.

'I didn't remember anything! I had even forgotten my four beloved hairs! Puja reminded me. "Repeat after me," she would say. "Four hairs. Four hairs…" and I repeated after her, slowly relearning all the things and words that I had forgotten.

'I finally remembered how to talk, eat and walk. I remembered that I was Uncle Leo, I remembered where I had come from, and I remembered all my adventures. That's how I recovered from the blow to my head. I was sure I had remembered everything.

'Now I could continue on my way. I went to Puja and told her, "Thank you, Puja! You saved my life! If you hadn't taken me into your home, I would have died on Hole Mountain and no one would have found me. Thanks to you, I've remembered everything I'd forgotten."

'But I knew that words weren't enough. I also wanted to help Puja. *How can I help Puja after all she has done for me?* I thought and thought, and while I was thinking I stuck my hand in my pocket and felt something inside. I took my hand out and saw a gold coin. I didn't know how the gold coin had got into my pocket. I didn't remember that I had found it on Hole Mountain. I didn't remember *anything* about the treasure I had found there!

"What does it matter where the coin is from?" I said to myself. "The important thing is to buy a present for Puja." I rushed to the marketplace to look for a nice gift for Puja. Suddenly, at one of the stalls, I noticed a blue dress—a new, clean dress without any holes.

'I saw the blue dress and felt funny. I felt like I was remembering something—something blue, something blue and important.

"What could it be?" I cried. But I couldn't remember. *Oh well*, I thought to myself, *it probably isn't very important. The important thing is that this dress is a wonderful present for Puja!*

'I bought the dress with the gold coin and went back

to Puja's cardboard house. I gave Puja the dress and told her, "You helped me. You saved my life. This dress is the least I can give you before we say goodbye."

'Puja was very excited. Puja's parents were happy as well. The blue dress was the first new piece of clothing that had ever been bought for her in her life. Puja put on the blue dress, and when I saw her in the dress, I thought, *Blue…blue rock…there was a rock that was blue like that dress. But what does that mean?* I couldn't remember. "It probably isn't very important," I told myself. I waved goodbye to the family and left.

'After parting ways with Puja, I couldn't stop thinking about a blue rock. I thought and thought and suddenly said to myself, "The pit with the blue rock…but which pit?" I couldn't remember. "It probably isn't very important," I told myself again, and walked away.' Uncle Leo fell silent and took a sip of his tea.

'Wait! Uncle Leo,' I said, 'didn't you remember the pit with the blue rock?'

Uncle Leo continued. 'I walked and walked. But only an hour later did I remember: "The pit with the blue rock! There's a marvellous treasure inside!" I cried. I ran back to the cardboard house.

"'Listen!" I said. "I've suddenly remembered the hiding place of an incredible treasure!" Puja's eyes opened wide. "Show me exactly where you found me," I told Puja.

'Puja, along with her parents, took me to the place where she had found me. I quickly noticed a blue rock resting by a pit. We went into the pit and found the chest filled with gold. I turned to Puja and her parents and told them, "Take the treasure. It's all yours."

"'Really?" cried the mother. "Thank you! With such a treasure we'll be able to eat a potato with sour cream every day!"

"'What are you talking about!" said the father. "With such a treasure we'll be able to *shower* in sour cream!"

'The whole family thanked me excitedly, and I went on my way.'

'And you didn't want the treasure for yourself?' I asked.

'Look,' said Uncle Leo, 'I wanted to help the little girl who had helped me. And in any case, I couldn't have continued with my other adventures with such a heavy treasure. And if I didn't go on adventures, I wouldn't have anything to tell you.'

'So maybe it's a good thing that you didn't take the treasure,' I said.

At dinner Mom said to me, 'Never mind that you didn't remember your part in the show. It happens sometimes.'

'He forgot it in front of the whole school!' said Graham. 'It was so embarrassing!'

'Stop that!' I snapped.

'It isn't such a big deal,' said Mom. 'Once I forgot my lines in a show too. It happens. It's not so terrible.'

'In front of the whole school?' I asked.

'Yes,' said Mom.

Dad came into the kitchen. 'I can't remember where I put my glasses. Have you seen them?' he asked Mom and kept looking.

'Did you know that Uncle Leo forgot everything when he was in the West Pole?' I said.

'Uncle Leo forgot everything?' said Dad as he kept on looking.

'Yes,' I said. 'He didn't even remember how to talk. But a little girl reminded him how to do everything again.'

Dad continued searching for his glasses. 'Where could I have put those glasses?' he wailed.

'Maybe that's what happened to you too?' I said to Dad. 'Like Uncle Leo.'

'That certainly might be the case,' Mom said, and she moved the kitchen towel. Dad's glasses were underneath it.

Uncle Leo, Half-Man-Half-Woman

On the following Wednesday, we were down in the yard of our building and Graham was playing soccer with his friends. Suddenly he called out and asked, 'Do you want to play with us?'

'Me?' I asked in surprise. Graham and his friends never invited me to play soccer. To tell you the truth, I don't even like soccer. Actually, I'm just bad at soccer. But I agreed to join.

'You be the goalie,' Graham said.

I stood in the goal and tried to watch the ball so I could stop it in time. But when the ball was kicked, it took me by surprise. It rolled quickly, passed between

Uncle Leo, Half-Man-Half-Woman 21

my feet, and went in.

'Why can't you stop such an easy kick?' Graham yelled at me. 'They scored because of you!'

At first I didn't know what to say, but then I shouted, 'So what if they scored? It's just a dumb game! And I don't even like soccer!'

'You don't like soccer? What are you, a girl?'

'I'm not a girl and I don't like soccer!'

'Only girls don't like soccer,' said Graham.

'That's stupid! There are girls who like soccer, and boys who don't, like me!' I shouted and went home.

When I went into the house, I found Uncle Leo already there. 'Uncle Leo,' I said. 'Do you know how to play soccer?'

'I'm not good at soccer,' said Uncle Leo.

'But do you like soccer?' I asked.

'I like the ball's round shape,' said Uncle Leo. 'And I like the green grass.'

'Graham says that boys always like soccer,' I said.

'So maybe I don't like soccer because I used to be half woman,' said Uncle Leo.

'*What?* You used to be half woman? When?'

'When I was visiting the Unfarious tribe,' said Uncle Leo.

'Unfreeze—what?'

'Unfarious. One da[y] wildest regions of the W of a tribe of cowboys. I all the women and all th on the sides of the road. but skinny. Skinny as rail[s]

'"Excuse me," I said everyone here so thin?"

'The man didn't say an little. I realized he was so

'I kept on walking. I the head of the tribe. H his tent. He was so weak have the strength to sit u

'"Hello," I said. "I'm everyone here so thin? W

'"Sir, it's all because o[f] feeble, whiny voice.

'"Chowzie?" I said. "V

'"Chowzie steals all of thin because of it!" said ate our cows and horses!'

'"Who is this Chowzie?" I asked.

'"Chowzie is a strange creature, sir," said the sheriff. "It's part man and part woman, part male dog and part female dog, part male cat and part female cat, part boat and part pot."

'"Have you tried to convince Chowzie to stop? Or tried to fight it?" I asked.

'"We've tried. We've tried *everything*," said the sheriff. "Chowzie can't be beaten because it has special powers. In fact, due to its powers, no man or woman can ever defeat it. No matter what weapon or method you use to fight it, whether you're a man or a woman, a boy or a girl, you can never beat the terrible Chowzie!" said the sheriff, adding, "I'm so hungry!"

'I was sorry to hear that Chowzie was stealing the cowboy tribe's food. I was sorry that everyone was so thin and weak. I thought, *Who can beat Chowzie? Only someone who is not a man and not a woman, not male and not female. But there's no such thing! So what can be done?*

I thought and thought and thought, and was sure that I couldn't find a solution when I suddenly came up with an idea. I had to tell my idea to the sheriff. I rushed back over to his tent. "I have an idea about how to beat

Chowzie!" I shouted excitedly.

'The sheriff mumbled, "There's no such idea...there's no such idea..."

"'Wait!' I said. "Just listen to my idea. I know this wonderful sorcerer. He once turned me into a cockroach. At first I was scared. I didn't want to be a cockroach, but in the end, I understood that life as a cockroach is great."

"'I would eat even a cockroach right now,' mumbled the sheriff. "Do you have a cockroach, by any chance, sir?"

"'Hold on,' I said. "That's not the whole story. If this sorcerer could turn me into a cockroach, he could probably turn one of you into part man and part woman. Chowzie won't be able to beat someone who's neither male nor female. It's an excellent idea, isn't it?"

'The sheriff looked at me tiredly. I thought he was going to faint, but then his eyes lit up and he said in a hoarse voice, "Great idea! But how do we get to this sorcerer?"

"'The sorcerer lives in the Romanian steppes," I said. "We'll send him a letter and ask for his help."

"'By the time the letter arrives...it will take a long time. By then we'll all have starved to death!" the sheriff said and started crying.

'But before the sheriff had even cried three tears, the

sorcerer suddenly appeared in front of us. "Did someone call for me?" he asked.

"'How did you get here so fast? How did you know we need your help?'

"'What do you mean?" said the sorcerer. "I'm a sorcerer. I know magic. And I always know when someone is talking about me."

"'Dear sorcerer,' I said. 'I'm Uncle Leo. Do you remember me? Once, in the Romanian steppes, you had turned me into a cockroach.'

"'A cockroach? Uncle Leo?" said the sorcerer. "In the Romanian steppes? Ah! Yes, yes! Now I remember. I won't change you into a cockroach again even if you beg me!"

"'No, no, this is about something else,' I said. 'This is the head of the Unfarious tribe. The tribe has a difficult problem, and only you can help. Chowzie is stealing all their food. If they don't beat it soon, everyone here will die of hunger. Chowzie has special powers: no man and no woman can beat it, no girl and no boy, no male and no female. So I thought that if you changed someone into a half-man–half-woman, they could beat Chowzie. Can you help?'

"'Ha-hee-hee-ha-ha!" laughed the sorcerer. "Gladly!"

he said, and then disappeared.

'I was very disappointed by the sorcerer's attitude. "I'm sorry," I told the sheriff. "I thought he would help, but…" I stopped talking because I saw the sheriff looking at me with amazement.

'"What's wrong?" I asked.

'The sheriff continued looking at me but seemed unable to speak. He didn't take his eyes off me. I didn't understand why he was staring.

'"Do I have dirt on my face?" I asked. "Are my hairs uncombed?"

'The sheriff shook his head. "He…he…the sorcerer…he changed you…" said the sheriff, and then he pulled out a small mirror from his pocket. I looked in the mirror and was shocked. The sorcerer had turned *me* into a half-man–half-woman! The right side of my face and body looked like they'd always looked, but the left side had turned into a woman. That wasn't what I wanted. That hadn't been the plan. I didn't mean for the sorcerer to turn *me* into a half-man–half-woman! I didn't know what to do.

'"The sorcerer really did it!" cried the head of the Unfarious tribe. "You're a half-man–half-woman! You're going to beat Chowzie! You, sir, I mean ma'am, I mean

sir-ma'am—never mind! What's important is that both of you are going to beat Chowzie!"

'"Why on earth should *I* fight it?' I cried.

'"You *have* to help us, or we'll all die of hunger!" replied the sheriff.

'I didn't know what to do. After a moment, I told myself, "If I've already turned into a half-man–half-woman, I might as well help the Unfarians."

'Wait a second, Uncle Leo,' I said. 'Did you really turn into a half-man–half-woman all over your body? Top and bottom?'

'Top and bottom, inside and out,' Uncle Leo said and continued with his story. 'I promised the sheriff that I would fight the terrible Chowzie the next morning. But that night, I lay in bed shaking with fear. I was afraid to fight it. They said Chowzie was gigantic. They said it was cruel. I didn't know if my idea would work. I didn't know if I could really beat it. The more I thought about it, the more anxious I became. But then, suddenly, I heard a woman's voice saying, "What are you so scared of? I'm sure we'll beat this Chowzie!"

'At first I couldn't understand who was talking to me. I looked around but didn't see anyone.

"'I'm not scared at all!" said the woman's voice. And then I understood that my female half was talking to me.

"'Are you sure?" my male half asked my female half.

"'One hundred percent sure!" said my female half.

'Her words encouraged me. "By the way," said my male half. "My name is Uncle Leo."

"'I know. I'm you. You're me. I'm half and you're half. Together we're one. I know everything you're thinking, and you know everything I'm thinking. And by the way, I want people to call us Aunt Leona."

"'Aunt Leona?" I asked. "Why?"

"'Why should we have a man's name and not a woman's name? Why is the male half more important?"

'Aunt Leona had a point, but my male half didn't want to give up his familiar name, Uncle Leo, so he said, "Let's discuss it in the morning."

'In the morning, I woke up to the sound of Aunt Leona's thoughts. She said, "I'm shaking with fear. Yesterday I thought fighting Chowzie would be a piece of cake. Today, I'm really scared! There's no way we'll win!"

"'Don't be scared. It'll be all right. Chowzie can beat a man or a woman. We're neither man nor woman. We're *both* man and woman. We're a winning combination!" I encouraged Aunt Leona and she calmed down.

'I got out of bed. I mean, both Aunt Leona and I got out of bed in one body and we went off to fight the frightening Chowzie. We left the tribe's camp and reached the place where Chowzie was hiding. It wasn't hard to find it. From a distance, we could already see the mountain of food Chowzie had stolen. It was a giant mountain, and next to it sat Chowzie, eating, chewing, swallowing, and making noises—*pak-pak-pak-pak-pak-pak! Tak-tak-tak-tak-tak-tak!*'

'"Oh my!" cried my male half. "It's so scary! It is really odd—part man and part woman, part male dog and part female dog, part male cat and part female cat, part boat and part pot. How frightening! Chowzie will eat us alive!"

'"Don't be scared," said Aunt Leona. "Let's go."

'We made our way towards Chowzie. We knew we'd be fighting it in another minute, but we didn't know how to fight it. We hid behind a boulder.

'My male half called out, "Chowzie! Return all the food you stole!"

'"You're welcome to come and take it!" Chowzie yelled and then laughed. "You haven't got a chance. You're just another man that I'll beat!"

'My female half called out, "Chowzie! Give back all the food you stole!"

'"You're welcome to come and take it!" Chowzie yelled and then laughed. "You haven't got a chance. You're just another woman that I'll beat!" It started singing:

Man or woman, girl or boy,
Come and give me tremendous joy.
I'll swallow you like a little bean,
In the greatest feast you've ever seen!

'As Chowzie sang, we moved closer. Suddenly Chowzie saw us. Its mean eyes opened wide. Its jaw dropped. I thought it would eat us like a bean any second!' Uncle Leo said and covered his face with his hands.

'Uncle Leo,' I said, 'what did Chowzie do to you?'

'As soon as Chowzie saw us, it cried out, "Oh, no! Not a man and not a woman! *Both* a man and a woman!" And it ran away screaming.'

'What? Chowzie just ran away as soon as it saw you? I mean, both of you?' I asked.

'That's right. As a half-man–half-woman, we didn't even have to fight it. Chowzie just ran away and didn't come back,' said Uncle Leo and continued with the story.

'We sighed in relief. We were happy we had won. We went back to the Unfarious tribe's camp and all the tribe members rejoiced. The sheriff was also happy that we had beat Chowzie. Everyone was glad to eat again. But then the sheriff turned to me and said, "Listen sir…ma'am… we aren't used to creatures, I mean, people like you, sir… ma'am. We don't want our children to see such things… If you two could leave, I'd really appreciate it."

'"Now that we've helped you, you're kicking us out?" Aunt Leona said in disbelief to the sheriff.

'"Please understand. We can't have a man, I mean a woman…I mean someone like you…living here. After all, it's pretty disgusting."

'We were very disappointed by the sheriff's request, but we left the camp.

'"How ungrateful!" said Aunt Leona angrily. "Despite our help, they treat us like we're not even human."

'"Never mind," my male half said, trying to calm her down.

'We kept on hiking through the West Pole. We lived together, we did everything together. I discovered there are advantages to being a half-man–half-woman:

'I could sing duets.

'I could dance the tango with myself.

'I always had someone to talk to.

'The days passed, and I got used to being a half-man–half-woman.

'"Aunt Leona, I never want to be separated from you," my male half said to my female half one morning.

'"I feel the same way," said my female half. "I can't imagine my life without you. Like you said, we're a winning combination!"

'But then one day, the sorcerer returned.

'"I've come to turn you back into a whole man!" he announced.

'"What are you talking about?" I cried. "Why did you come back? I thought you had forgotten about me!"

'"I didn't forget. I just was busy with other magical deeds. Now I'll remove your female half!"

'"No! Please! Don't!" we cried. "We want to stay together! We've gotten used to each other. We feel like this is what we want to be!"

'"There's no choice," said the sorcerer. "This is a temporary spell, and you can't make a temporary spell permanent!"

'"Then…then remove me, the male half!" begged my

male half. "I'm willing to be a whole woman!"

"'This isn't a customized magic service!" said the sorcerer, annoyed "I'm cancelling the temporary spell. Turning you into a woman is a whole different spell, and I have no reason to do it!"

"'Just a minute! Wait!" my male half called out. "Let us say goodbye!"

'The sorcerer waited, and my male half said to Aunt Leona, "We are about to be separated. You have been a part of me. We've been through so much together. You completed me. I have never felt more whole. You are brave and wise. I will never forget you."

Then the sorcerer spat out a few magic words, turned me back into a whole Uncle Leo, and disappeared.

'I stood there all alone. I was Uncle Leo again, the way I had been born. But let me tell you this, Andy—to this day, I still miss Aunt Leona!' said Uncle Leo, and I could see the longing in his eyes.

Uncle Leo's adventure was sad, but I was happy that in the end, Uncle Leo had stayed Uncle Leo.

'By the way, Aunt Leona liked soccer very much,' he said.

'Really?' I asked.

'Yes. If she hadn't been attached to me, she probably would have been an excellent player.'

At dinner that night, Graham sat at the table with a medal hanging around his neck. He had won it in an after-school soccer game. He talked about the game throughout the entire meal.

'I think we're going to win the championships next year,' he said. 'Coach says that if we work hard, we can do it.'

I looked at Graham's medal. I didn't like soccer, but it would be nice if I had a medal, too.

Phoebe came into the kitchen. She was holding a ball in her hand and tried to throw it to Mom. The ball fell and rolled under the table.

'Graham, maybe next year Phoebe can join your team?' asked Mom.

'No way!' said Graham. 'She's too little. And besides, she's a girl.'

'So what?' said Mom.

'Girls don't play soccer,' said Graham.

'That's not true!' I said. 'When Uncle Leo was a half-man–half-woman, his female half was a really great soccer player.'

'What?' asked Dad. 'Uncle Leo's female half?'

'Yes,' I said. 'Her name was Aunt Leona. She was a champion at soccer. The problem was that she was attached to Uncle Leo, and Uncle Leo is a terrible soccer player.'

'In short,' said Mom. 'I think Phoebe would make an excellent soccer player.'

'Exactly like her father,' said Dad, trying to pass the ball to Phoebe. The ball bounced on to the table, hit a glass, and spilled juice all over his shirt.

'Yes, exactly,' said Mom, smiling.

Uncle Leo in Professor Scientifani's Lab

Graham has a friend from his after-school soccer team. His name is Roy. He comes over sometimes. To tell you the truth, I don't really like it when Roy comes over, because when he visits us, Graham isn't very nice. Of course, there are lots of times when my brother isn't nice to me, but when Roy's there, Graham becomes even meaner.

When Roy came over on Wednesday, Graham asked me if I wanted to play checkers with them. Roy suggested we have a tournamen—the winner of each game would get to keep playing while the loser would be replaced. I was happy to join, because I really like checkers. I thought it would be fun to play with my brother and Roy, but I didn't actually enjoy it at all. I lost the first game I played.

'You're really bad!' Graham told me.

I didn't know what to say, so I kept quiet.

The next game I played was with Roy. I lost again.

'What's wrong with you? Don't you see what you have to do?' Graham said to me. 'Don't you have any brains?'

'Stop it!' I shouted. 'Just cut it out!' I really hate it when my brother tells me I don't have any brains.

After that, Roy and Graham played another game, and then I played again and lost again. Graham started singing, 'Andy, the baby, is dumb as a wall, he doesn't have any brains at all! Andy, the baby, is dumb as a wall, he doesn't have any brains at all!'

I asked Graham to stop, but it didn't help. In the end, he and Roy went off to their soccer practice, and I was left by myself. I sat in the living room. I knew that my brother was just teasing me, but I was still worried. Maybe there really *was* something wrong with my brain. Maybe it was too small! Maybe it didn't work right.

I was sitting in the living room, worrying about my brain, when Uncle Leo came in. He sat down on the couch.

'Uncle Leo,' I asked, 'is it possible that I have a problem

with my brain?'

'A problem with your brain?' said Uncle Leo. 'I don't think so. Why do you ask?'

'I'm not good at a lot of things. I think there's something wrong with my brain.'

Uncle Leo looked at me thoughtfully. 'I know what you're talking about,' he said. 'I was once told that I have no brain at all.'

'You were told that too? Who said it?'

'Professor Scientifani,' said Uncle Leo.

'Who? Professor what?'

'Scientifani,' said Uncle Leo. 'I'll tell you about it. While I was travelling in the westernmost regions of the West Pole, where the sun sets twenty-four hours a day, I was searching for the twilight flower. I really wanted to see this flower because I had been told that it's both enormous and beautiful. I searched and searched and finally saw the flower way off in the distance. It was huge. It was the biggest flower I had ever seen in my life. It was as tall as a building. I got closer to it. It gave off a strong fragrance, a wonderful sweet smell. The stem was as thick as a tree trunk. I started to climb it. I climbed higher and higher, but then out of the blue, a giant net came down all around me. I was startled. I tried to escape, but couldn't. I was trapped inside!

'Suddenly, I heard a shout. "Got it!"

'"What is it, Professor Scientifani?" asked another voice.

'I looked up and saw two enormous monkeys staring at me. They were the ones who had spoken. They were the ones who had caught me in the huge net. I looked at them in alarm. Their eyes were so big that they looked like huge lakes. Their noses were immense. The nostrils looked like caves. Next to these two gigantic monkeys, I was teeny—the size of a fly.

'"I don't know what it is. I've never seen a bug like this before," said the huge Professor Scientifani. "We'll take it to the laboratory and study it." Then she picked me up with a pair of tongs and put me inside a jar.

'"Wait!" I shouted. "What are you doing? Let me go! Why are you putting me in a jar?" But the two giant monkeys didn't hear me. Compared to them, I was tiny. My voice was so thin and small that their big ears couldn't hear me.

'The two hairy scientists brought me to their lab. It was full of gigantic microscopes, strange test tubes and

instruments. The walls were decorated with countless tubes and jars holding all sorts of animals—elephants, giraffes, lions and more. All of the animals were dead. I looked at the dead animals and got really scared. I didn't want to end up as a lab decoration.

'Professor Scientifani took me out of the jar and placed me under a microscope.

'"Dr Sentimentani, bring me a test tube," she said to the monkey standing next to her. I understood that he was her assistant.

'Professor Scientifani looked into the microscope and let out a scream. "What is this? I've never seen a bug like this before!"

'"I'm not a bug! I'm a human being! A h-u-m-a-n!" I cried with all my might, but the professor didn't hear me.

'"Dr Sentimentani, come here. Look what a strange bug this is," said Scientifani to her assistant.

'The assistant came up to the microscope, peered into it, and said, "A strange bug indeed. I think we've found a new bug that no one knows about! How great! This is a wonderful discovery!"

'"*We've* found? What do you mean—we?" spat Scientifani, baring her large teeth. "I found it! I discovered it! You're just my assistant. Don't ever forget that!"

'Sentimentani didn't answer.

"'Now write down everything I tell you," Scientifani instructed Sentimentani. She looked at me through the microscope and said, "I see that it has four little legs."

'Sentimentani wrote it down, and I called out, "Those aren't legs! Those are my four hairs!" But they didn't hear me, of course.

"'I see that in the middle of its body there is a soft ball which it probably uses to roll around and move from place to place."

"'Wrong!" I called. "That's my round pot belly!" But they didn't hear me.

"'The creature's ball then splits into two parts shaped like tweezers. It uses these to prey on smaller creatures and then eats them," said Scientifani.

"'That's not true!" I yelled. "I don't prey on anyone! These are my legs. They aren't tweezers. I walk on these legs!" But my voice wasn't heard.

"'On each side of its body are wings that fell into disuse over years of evolution. Its ancestors probably knew how to fly," said Scientifani.

"'I wish I had wings!" I shouted. "These are my arms!"

But it didn't help.

"'Based on all the data before us," summed up Professor Scientifani, "this is a brainless bug that is not capable of thinking, cannot talk, and does not feel anything. It is not beautiful in the slightest, and its contribution to the animal world is unclear. And that, in fact, is what makes it unique."

"'I *do* have a brain!" I yelled. "I can talk, but you don't hear me! I can think! I don't know if I'm beautiful, and I don't know if I contribute anything to the animal world, but on all other accounts you're completely wrong!"

'Dr Sentimentani wrote down everything Professor Scientifani said. Then Scientifani put me back inside the jar and said, "This is a marvellous discovery! The whole science world is going to be excited about it!" She was so enthusiastic that her fur bristled. She lifted the jar, and I tried to wave and signal to her that I wasn't a bug, that I didn't want to stay in the jar, and could she please set me free.

"'Look at how it's trying to fly," said Scientifani to Sentimentani. "But it doesn't have a chance, its wings are useless. Well, we're done for today. Put it in the refrigerator for the night."

'Sentimentani took the jar, put it in the refrigerator, and closed the door. I sat in the jar inside the refrigerator, in the dark. I wanted to escape, but couldn't climb out of the jar. I didn't know what to do. Suddenly, I noticed a crow in the jar next to me.

'"Excuse me! Crow!" I called. The crow looked at me in despair.

'"Crow," I said, "maybe we can escape by working together?"

'"Escape? Finito, there's no way!" said the crow in a quiet voice. "We are trapped here until tomorrow morning. Tomorrow morning they will take us out and operate on us. Nothing can be done. Good night."

'The crow folded his wings sadly and closed his eyes.

'"Operate?" I yelled in a panic. "They're going to cut up my body? Oh, no!"

'I understood that the next day, the two scientists would take me out of the refrigerator and dissect me

to continue studying me. I don't think they cared that it would hurt me. I don't think they cared whether I survived or died.

'I sat in the jar, frightened and worried. The refrigerator was cold and dark. I started shaking. I thought I would die of cold!' said Uncle Leo, hugging himself.

'But, Uncle Leo,' I said, 'didn't you manage to get out of the refrigerator?'

'I didn't know how I could get out,' said Uncle Leo. 'I sat in the jar. I don't know how much time passed, but suddenly the refrigerator door opened. The light went on, and I saw Dr Sentimentani, the assistant. He was alone. He took the jar out of the refrigerator.

'"What are you planning to do?" I called.

'Sentimentani didn't hear me. He took me out of the jar and placed me under the microscope lens again.

'"That Professor Scientifani thinks she's the smartest ape in the world," he said. I didn't understand who he was talking to. "She thinks that only she deserves all the credit. But we found it together. So why should she get all the glory? Why should this discovery be only hers?" Sentimentani kept on talking, and since there was no one else in the room, I understood that he was talking to himself. Of course, it never occurred to him that I could hear him.

'Dr Sentimentani looked at me under the microscope. I tried to call out to him, but he didn't notice.

"'I'll cut it into four pieces. Then I'll study each piece carefully," said Sentimentani. "*I'll* write an article about it! *I'll* win the glory!" he exclaimed, lifting his tail and coming at me with a scalpel,' Uncle Leo said, squeezing his lips together tightly.

'Uncle Leo,' I said, 'did Sentimentani really dissect you?'

Uncle Leo continued with his story. 'Sentimentani approached me with the knife. I screamed at the top of my lungs, "No! No! Dr Sentimentani! Listen to me! I'm a human. I'm not a bug. I know how to think and talk!"

'Dr Sentimentani stopped. He moved the knife away from me and said, "What's this? What's going on here? I need to get look closely." He moved the lens of the microscope closer to me. I kept yelling and Sentimentani said, "This is strange, very strange. I think it has a mouth! If it has a mouth, perhaps it also talks, and if it talks, perhaps it thinks, and if it thinks, evidently it has a brain. Is it possible that the grand Professor Scientifani was wrong about everything she said?"

"'Yes!" I shouted. "She *was* wrong! She was completely wrong!"

'Sentimentani caught me with the tongs and laid me on a vial.

"'What are you going to do to me?" I asked, scared.

'He took a mini microphone and put it close to me.

"'I'm a human being!" I called, and heard my voice echoing in the room.

"'A human?" wondered Sentimentani.

"'Yes. I'm not a bug," I said. "I can talk and I can think. And I don't have four legs—those are my four hairs. I don't have a ball that I move on—that's my stomach. And I have a brain!"

"'Amazing! Amazing! Such a tiny creature that can talk and think. How fortunate that I put a microphone beside it. This is a marvellous discovery! I will publish it in a special article, and all the scientists will look up to me. This is a scientific revolution!" Sentimentani was excited and moved his eyebrows up and down. "Now I just have to dissect it in order to understand what's inside its body!"

"'No!" I yelled. "Please don't dissect me!"

'Sentimentani looked at me in wonder, and his nostrils flared. "I'm sorry," he said. "It's part of scientific research." That was the first time he had talked directly to me.

"But I'm begging you. It would hurt me. I'd die!"

"It's all for the sake of science. For the sake of progress. For research, for the article, for the worldwide fame I will receive. You must agree that these are great reasons for dissecting you."

'Sentimentani took the scalpel and came at me again. He intended to cut me up to study me and examine what was inside my body. I didn't know what to do.

"I'll tell you what's in my body!" I shouted. "You don't have to cut me!"

"I have to see it with my own eyes!" said Sentimentani.

"Hold on, wait!" I cried. "If you don't operate on me, I'll tell you stories!"

"Stories?" said Sentimentani.

"Marvellous stories," I said. "Wonderful adventures. Just think—you can write about these adventures in your article."

'Sentimentani thought for a moment and then said, "Great idea! The article will come out longer. Maybe it will even be a book! Tell me, I'm writing everything down."

'And so I told Dr Sentimentani stories.'

'What did you tell him?' I asked.

'I told him about how I forgot everything at Hole Mountain and how I turned into a half-man–half-woman and fought Chowzie. I told him about other adventures from all sorts of places that I've visited. Sentimentani wrote everything down, and then he said with a smile, "I'm not going to dissect you. I'm going to take you to my lectures. Your stories are wonderful. Many people will want to hear them. Not just scientists. Everyone will want to hear them. Masses of people will come to my lectures, and I'll be the richest and most famous scientist in the world!"

'I sighed with relief. I was glad that Sentimentani wasn't going to dissect me. I was glad my life had been saved.

'"I'll name you *Sentimentus adventurius*, after me," said Sentimentani.

'"Actually, I already have a name," I said. "My name is Uncle Leo."

'"Uncle Leo? So maybe *Uncle Leo sentimentus*? It doesn't matter right now. We have to hurry up and get out of here before Professor Scientifani arrives. She'll want to cut you up and steal my scientific discovery," said Sentimentani, putting me in the jar and taking me with him.

'And indeed, I started telling my adventures at Sentimentani's lectures. Everyone listened and enjoyed them. Sentimentani became a very famous scientist. No one had ever imagined that there were such tiny creatures that are capable of thinking, talking and even telling interesting stories. Everybody wanted to hear them.

'Although I enjoyed sharing my adventures, I didn't want to spend my whole life as Dr Sentimentani's lab animal. I wanted to continue on my way. But Sentimentani made sure I wouldn't run away.

'I slept in his lab at nights. He would feed me and let me drink, but he didn't agree to set me free. I didn't know what to do,' said Uncle Leo, raising both his hands.

'Uncle Leo,' I said, 'how did you manage to get away?'

'I was sure I would never manage to escape. But then one night, I was woken up by noises in Sentimentani's lab. The light went on, and suddenly I saw Professor Scientifani. She was opening all the cages and jars and setting all the animals free.

'"This will teach that Sentimentani a lesson!" screamed Scientifani. "This will stop him from researching behind my back!"

'I was sure that any moment, she would come up to me and release me. I was happy. Professor Scientifani came closer. I thought I would be set free, but then I noticed that Scientifani was holding a giant burning match in her hand.

'"What are you going to do with that match?" I cried.

'"I'm going to burn you up!" shouted Scientifani, baring her teeth. "Sentimentani won't be able to take you to any more lectures! No one will be able to hear your stories!"

'Scientifani brought the match closer to me. Compared to my body, the flame was enormous. I knew that as soon as it got near me, I would burn up like a moth. But at the last second I called out, "Wait! I have an idea that will help you publish a marvellous scientific discovery!"

'Scientifani stopped in her tracks. "What idea could I possibly hear from a creature that has no brain?" she asked.

'"Please listen," I said. "I'm willing to sign a letter saying that I have no brains, that I can't talk, that I can't think, that I'm a bug that makes no contribution to the world. In exchange, you have to promise me that you won't burn or dissect me, but you will set me free."

'Scientifani thought about my suggestion and said, "Great idea! That way, I can show the world that Sentimentani was wrong and I was right!"

'She blew out the match, put a giant piece of paper on the table and wrote this on it:

> I, the undersigned, hereby proclaim that I make no contribution to the world. I have no brains, and I am not capable of thinking or talking. I have no feelings and I have never told any stories—interesting or otherwise. Also, I do not have four hairs but four legs.

Scientifani handed me a huge pen. I held it with both hands and signed at the bottom of the page. Then Scientifani took me out of the lab. She said, "Thank you, Uncle Leo. Now I will be world famous because of you!' She set me free and I walked away."

'But, Uncle Leo,' I said, 'you *do* have a brain! Why did you sign the letter?'

'Lucky for me that I have a brain, so I used it to get away from Sentimentani and Scientifani,' said Uncle Leo.

'It's really lucky that you got away from them,' I said.

'Yes,' said Uncle Leo. 'That was an adventure that I

successfully got out of. But there's an adventure that I've never yet been free of to this day.'

I looked at Uncle Leo. I didn't understand what he meant.

'I'll tell you about that adventure next week,' he promised.

At dinner, Dad, Phoebe and I sat at the table. We were waiting for Graham and Mom to come home. I didn't eat. I had no appetite. Dad had just told me that Graham had broken his leg at soccer practice, and Mom had taken him to the hospital. I was really worried.

When Graham and Mom walked into the house, I saw that Graham's leg was in a cast. Mom was helping him walk, and he sat down on the couch in the living room.

Dad went over to him. 'Does it still hurt?' he asked Graham.

'Yes,' said Graham. He wasn't crying now, but I could tell from his voice that he had been crying before.

'Graham was so brave at the hospital,' said Mom.

'The doctor asked me to move my leg, and it hurt a

lot,' Graham told us. 'And then they took an X-ray, and then about eight different doctors checked me. And then they put the cast on and they wanted to give me a tetanus shot but in the end they didn't.'

'Did they operate on you?' I asked.

'No,' said Graham. 'The doctor said it's not a severe fracture.'

'That's lucky,' I said. 'I was worried about you.'

'Really?' asked Graham.

'He was so worried that he didn't eat any supper,' said Dad.

'Well, now both of you can sit and eat,' said Mom. We all sat down to eat.

'The doctor said that people can sign my cast and draw on it, if I want them to,' Graham told me.

'But how will you play soccer?' I asked.

'I won't be playing any soccer, at least not until they take the cast off.'

'So next week, you can hear all about Uncle Leo's adventure!' I said.

'That'll be fun!' said Graham.

'How about that!' said Mom. 'We've already discovered one good thing about the cast.'

Uncle Leo Dreams On and On and On

The next week, Graham and I sat on the balcony, waiting for Uncle Leo. When he arrived, Graham asked him to sign his cast. Uncle Leo signed it, and then Graham said, 'Andy told me that you had an adventure that you've never managed to be free of. What did you mean when you said that?'

Uncle Leo sat down and told us. 'It all started after I left Scientifani and Sentimentani. I continued travelling through the West Pole. I walked and walked until I got tired. I looked for a place to eat and sleep, but I couldn't find any hotel or hostel. I was exhausted. My feet were begging me to lie down and rest. My eyelids were asking me to close my eyes and go to sleep. Suddenly, I saw a large tree on the side of the road. I lay down in its shade and quickly fell asleep.

'I slept under the tree and dreamed. I dreamed that I woke up, walked around the wide tree trunk, and found a door. On the door was a sign that said "No Entrance."

'Now, I ask you—what does one feel like doing when one stands in front of a door that says "No Entrance"?'

'Opening it and going inside,' Graham and I said at once.

'Exactly. I wanted to know what was on the other side of the door. I went up to the door and opened it cautiously. I found I could enter the tree trunk. I went in, and as soon as I was standing inside the tree, the door closed behind me with a slam. Everything was totally dark around me. I couldn't see a thing. I tried to find the door. I wanted to open it so some light would come in. I groped around, but I couldn't find the door. I didn't understand where it had disappeared to. I took a little step. I tried to touch the sides of the trunk from the inside, but even though I walked and walked, to my surprise, I didn't get anywhere and didn't see anything— only total darkness. I couldn't understand where I was and didn't know how to get out.

'All at once I saw a pair of eyes in the dark. The eyes looked at me. I looked at them.

'"Hello," I said quietly, but I got no reply. The eyes kept looking at me.

'"Excuse me," I said. "Where's the exit?"

'Suddenly the pair of eyes lit a torch. The torch lit up my surroundings, and I was surprised! I was shocked! I was astounded!' said Uncle Leo, and I saw through his glasses that his eyes had opened wide.

'Uncle Leo,' said Graham, 'what did you see?'

'I saw to whom the eyes belonged. I had thought that the eyes were in one head, but I was wrong. By the light of the torch, I saw *two* people were standing in front of me. One eye was on one head and the other eye was on the other head. Each of them had only one eye in the

middle of their forehead! I had never seen people like that. It really scared me.

'But there was more than just their appearance that was frightening. The moment the torch was lit, the two people started chasing me.

'"Hey! What are you doing here? Why have you entered our dream?" they called out angrily, trying to catch me.

'I started running away. I ran and ran, and the two people chased me calling, "Get out of our dream! This is *our* dream! Get out of our dream!"

'I escaped, and as I ran I thought, *This really is a dream. It's not really happening. I'm asleep, after all. I'm just dreaming. The best thing would be to simply wake up from this dream. I have to wake up!*

'I shook myself, but the two men and the two eyes kept chasing me. I didn't wake up. I pinched myself, but

the two men and the two eyes didn't disappear. I slapped myself, but the two eyes kept on glaring at me. I didn't wake up! I didn't know what to do. How could I wake up from this horrible dream?

'Eventually, I put my hand on my four hairs and pulled with all my might. It hurt a lot, and the men and the eyes and the darkness immediately vanished. I had finally woken up.

'I thought I would find myself under the tree where I had lain down to sleep in the shade. But surprisingly, I found myself in a completely different place,' said Uncle Leo, placing his hands on his cheeks.

'Where did you find yourself?' I asked. 'What happened, Uncle Leo?'

'I woke up in a hospital bed. I couldn't understand how I had got there. I thought that maybe I had been in an accident. Maybe I had been hurt and brought to the hospital in an ambulance. A nurse was standing with her back to me, arranging colorful candy in a bowl.

'"Excuse me, nurse," I said.

'She didn't turn towards me.

'"Excuse me, nurse, how did I get here?" I asked fearfully. "What happened to me?"

'The nurse turned to me, holding the bowl of candy. But her face was strange! She also had only one eye! I realized that I had woken up into another dream!

'"Don't worry," said the nurse. "You can eat all the candy." She put the bowl in front of me, and I started eating. They were delicious!

'"Well," I told myself. "Now this is a good dream. I've never tasted such good candy—either sleeping or awake." I was happy. I no longer wanted to wake up from this delicious dream. But then the nurse came over to me with a large syringe in her hand.

'"It's time to give you your medicine," she said.

'"Oh, no!" I cried. "Now this isn't a good dream any more!"

'I got out of the bed and started running away. I went out of the hospital to the street. The nurse disappeared. I looked around me. All the men, women and children had only one eye in the middle of their foreheads. But I was glad to see that the one-eyed people didn't chase me. I walked along the street, and people looked at me now and then with a curious look. They probably weren't used to seeing someone with two eyes.

'"How will I wake up from this dream?" I asked myself.

I thought and thought and thought until I got an idea. *I need a clock to wake up! I'll go buy an alarm clock, and it will wake me up.*

'Suddenly a woman spoke to me, saying, "If you're looking for a clock, go to the clockmaker."

"'Where is the clockmaker?" I asked.

"'He lives in the tall clock tower," said the woman, pointing at a clock tower.

'I thanked the woman and immediately walked to the tower. I climbed to the top and went into the clock shop. In the shop were innumerable clocks that ticked and tocked and tick-tocked. There were a great many clocks in the store and a great many tick-tocks. So the whole place was really noisy. I searched for the clockmaker among the clocks, but I couldn't find him.

"'Excuse me," I called out. "Is anyone here?" I could barely hear myself for all the tick-tocking. I was happy to see that the clockmaker heard me. He came out of a big clock standing in the corner. The clockmaker also had only one eye, and he wore a monocle on it.

"'Ho!" he said. "You've arrived just in time!"

"'Did you know that I was coming here?" I asked.

"'No," said the clockmaker. "But I have many clocks

here, and each clock shows a different time. So it doesn't matter when you arrive, because we'll surely be able to find at least one clock that shows that you came exactly on time." And then he asked with a smile, "How may I help you?"

"'I need an alarm clock,' I said.

"'Alarm? An alarm clock?" said the clockmaker. "What's an alarm clock?"

'I was surprised that the clockmaker had never heard of an alarm clock. "An alarm clock is a clock that you set to a certain hour and then you go to sleep. The clock rings at the time you set, and wakes you up from your sleep."

"'Why?" asked the clockmaker. "Why would you want a clock to wake you from sleeping? Why would anyone ever need a clock like that?" asked the clockmaker.

"'Because I have to wake up,' I said.

"'You look pretty awake right now,' said the clockmaker.

"'I look awake to you because you're in my dream,' I tried to explain. "I'm dreaming that I'm meeting you, but I'm actually asleep right now. I want to wake up from this dream."

"'You're not happy to meet me?" said the clockmaker.

'"No, no, of course I'm happy. It's a pleasure to meet you. But I just want to wake up. I need an alarm clock that will ring and wake me up," I tried to explain.

'The clockmaker looked at me in confusion. He didn't understand what I meant. Finally he said, "I only have a drowsy clock."

'"What's a drowsy clock?" I asked.

'"It's a clock that you set for a certain hour, and then it rings at that time, and as soon as you hear the ring, you fall asleep," the clockmaker explained.

'I didn't know what to do. I wanted a clock that would wake me up from my dream. What would I do with a clock that would put me to sleep? And what would happen if I fell asleep inside the dream instead of waking up? I didn't know what to do. Finally I said to the clockmaker, "Well, I'll try the drowsy clock. Maybe it will help me get out of this dream."

'The clockmaker sold me the drowsy clock. I left the shop. I sat down on a bench. I set the clock to ring one minute later. I placed the clock down next to me and waited,' said Uncle Leo, leaning back in the armchair.

'Uncle Leo,' asked Graham, 'what happened when the clock rang?'

'I'll tell you what happened,' said Uncle Leo. 'As soon as the clock rang, my eyes closed and I fell asleep. A while later, I opened my eyes and found myself lying under the big tree in whose shade I had lain down to sleep. I was so happy to be back at the tree.

'*I've woken up from the dream*, I thought. *Now I can go on travelling and maybe even return home.*

'I got off the ground. I stretched. I rubbed my eyes.

'"What a strange and scary dream I had!" I said to myself. "That strange door in the tree and the people with one eye... I have to check whether there's really a door in the tree." I circled the gigantic tree trunk and was surprised to discover that there was, in fact, a door in the tree. *That's funny*, I thought. *Was it a dream or reality?* I didn't know. This time, I didn't dare open the door. I continued on my way. I didn't know if I was dreaming or awake.

'I decided to go back home. I kept on marching until I reached a bus stop. I waited. When the bus arrived, I got on and paid the driver. The driver looked at me, and I saw he had only one eye. But still I rode the bus and continued travelling until I got home from the West Pole,' said Uncle Leo and fell silent.

'But, Uncle Leo,' I said, 'did you wake up from the dream in the end?'

'I didn't wake up from it,' said Uncle Leo.

'So you're still dreaming it? Even now?' I asked.

'Yes,' said Uncle Leo.

'And do you see people who have only one eye?' asked Graham.

'Sometimes.'

'And don't you want to wake up from this dream?' I asked.

'No, I don't want to wake up any more. If I can sit with you and tell you my adventures, that's a wonderful dream for me!' Uncle Leo said with a smile.

We smiled too.

'And by the way,' said Uncle Leo, 'I brought you what was left of the candy that the nurse in the hospital gave me.' Uncle Leo put his hand in his pocket, took out a handful of candy, and put them on the table. 'They're simply delicious,' he said.

After Uncle Leo left, Graham and I sat in the balcony, gobbling down candy that Uncle Leo had brought us from his dream.

'Uncle Leo's dream was really interesting,' said Graham.

'But actually, what we're saying now is also part of Uncle Leo's dream, isn't it?' I said.

'Yes,' said Graham. 'You're right!'

I was surprised. I couldn't remember my brother Graham ever saying I was right before. He always tells me that I'm wrong, that I can't do anything, that I have no talent. And now he was telling me that I was right. *Maybe this really is a dream,* I thought. But I didn't say anything.

Uncle Leo keeps visiting us every Wednesday and telling us his adventures. Graham had his cast taken off a long time ago, but sometimes, on Wednesdays, when he is supposed to play soccer, he asks Mom if he can stay home to hear Uncle Leo's fascinating adventures. He says he might even switch to a different after-school activity.